HARVEY THE HICCUPPING HIPPOPOTAMUS

by
Tanya Baker and Carlton Holm

Illustrations by Sue Wilkinson

BARRON'S

All inquiries should be addressed to:
Barron's Educational Series, Inc.
250 Wireless Boulevard
Hauppauge, NY 11788

International Standard Book No. 0-8120-6248-5 (hardcover)
International Standard Book No. 0-8120-4927-6 (paperback)

Library of Congress Catalog Card No. 91-35971

PRINTED IN HONG KONG
2345   9927   0987654321

This is Harvey the Hippopotamus.

Harvey has a problem. He has the hiccups, and he does not know how to get rid of them.

Just then, Harvey saw Frances the Forgetful Fish. "Frances, please help me get rid of these hiccups," he begged.

Frances thought for a moment and then said, "Harvey, you must drink water to get rid of these hiccups. That works for me."

So Harvey drank water, and he drank, and he drank, and he drank, and he drank…

And then…

Poor Harvey could not drink another drop of water, and he still had the hiccups.

Harvey had to find a cure for his hiccups, so he decided to leave the pond.

As he was leaving the pond, he met Bill the Bouncing Bullfrog.

Bill heard Harvey hiccup and said, "Harvey, I get rid of the hiccups by hopping on one foot. It always works! You should try that."

As you know, hippos are very large, and Harvey had never tried to jump on one foot before, but he was willing to try it.

Harvey slowly got on one foot.
Then he tried to jump, but nothing
happened. He just could not get off
the ground on one foot.

Finally Harvey said, "Thank you, Bill, for trying to help me, but I just cannot hop on one foot."

Bill hopped away, saying, "Good luck, Harvey. I hope you find some way to cure your hiccups."

HICCUP!

As Harvey walked further away from his pond, he met Tommie the Tiny Turtle.

Harvey asked, "Tommie, can you help me stop these hiccups, please?"

Tommie said, "Harvey, you hold your breath while I count to ten, and your hiccups will be gone."

"Ready," said Tommie.

Harvey nodded his head yes and took a deep breath, not knowing how slowly a turtle counts.

Tommie began

"O...N...E...

T...W...O...

T...H...R...E...E...

F...O...U...R...

F...I...V..E...

S...I...X...

S...E..V..E..N...

E...I...G...H...T...

N...I...N...E...

T...E...N..."

And then...

Harvey still had the hiccups.

He thanked Tommie anyway and left in search of some way of curing the hiccups.

He continued walking toward a small forest. As he walked, he met Freddy the Funny Fox. Harvey said, "Freddy, a fox is cunning and smart. You must know how to stop the hiccups!"

Freddy fluffed his tail and proudly replied, "Harvey, the only way to stop the hiccups is to say the alphabet backwards. It always works for me."

So, Harvey began,

**"Z, Y, X, W, V, U, T ,S, R, Q,
P, O, N, M, L, K, J, I, H,
G, F, E, D, C, B, A!"**

"I made it! I said the alphabet backwards!"

HICCUP!

But, still, Harvey had the hiccups.

He thanked Freddy and continued to walk in search of a cure.

As Harvey passed a paper sack in the grass, he heard, "I know how."

Harvey leaned down to look into the sack. It was KoKo the Curious Kitten.

She repeated, "I know how. I know how to get rid of the hiccups."

Harvey begged KoKo, "Please tell me how I can stop these hiccups."

"Harvey, you must take this sack and breathe in and out into it."

Harvey took the sack and breathed out,
blowing the sack out. Then he breathed in,
shrinking the sack.
   He did this several times without a single…

HICCUP!

Harvey still had not found a way to cure his hiccups.

He thanked KoKo and continued walking toward the small forest.

As Harvey walked under the tree, he heard a voice say, "To cure the hiccups, you must stand on your head."

Harvey looked up and saw Millie the Mischievous Monkey hanging upside down.

Millie said, "Harvey, if you stand on your head, the hiccups will just fall right out. I know because it works for me."

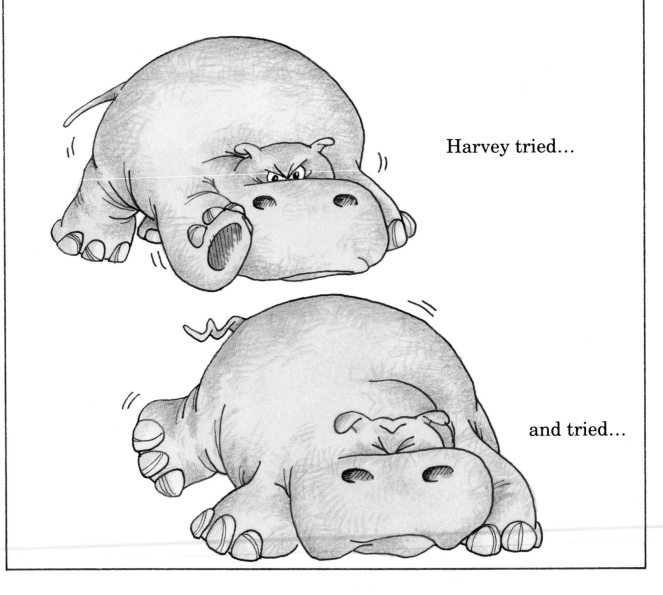

Harvey tried...

and tried...

and tried…

…and tried to stand on his head,
but he just could not do it!

Suddenly, Harvey felt a tickle. He looked down and saw a **HUGE SPIDER** crawling up his arm.

Harvey screamed,

AAAAA

GGGHHHHH!!!

and shook the spider off his arm.

As Harvey stood there, Sammy the Sneaky Spider said, "I knew I could cure your hiccups, Harvey. I scared them away!"

And, as Harvey looked at Sammy, he realized it was true.

The hiccups were gone!

At last someone had found the cure for his hiccups!